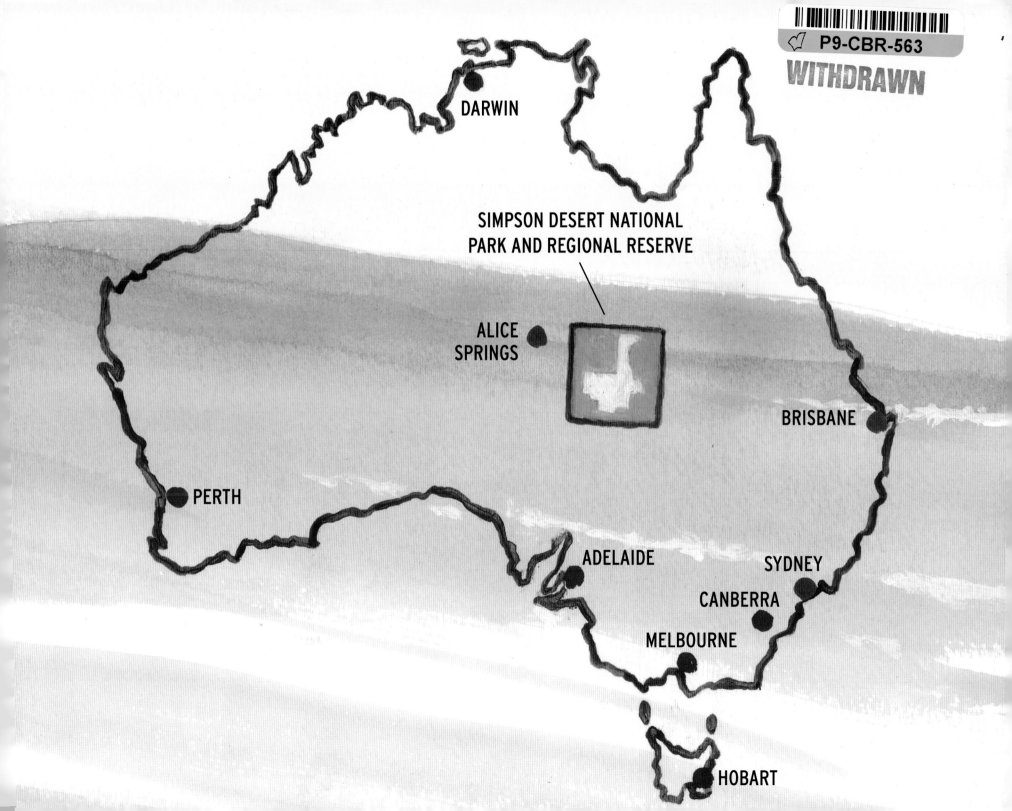

DARWIN

SIMPSON DESERT NATIONAL
PARK AND REGIONAL RESERVE

ALICE
SPRINGS

BRISBANE

PERTH

ADELAIDE

SYDNEY

CANBERRA

MELBOURNE

HOBART

To Chris, Bobby, Aaron, Nik, Anke, and Tony and the wonderful team of scientists and volunteers from the April 2010 Simpson Desert trip. Cheers to twenty years of research —D. M.

May children read and learn of the different places in the world — J. V. Z.

First published in the United States of America in July 2012 by Walker Publishing Company, Inc., a division of Bloomsbury Publishing, Inc.
www.bloomsburykids.com

For information about permission to reproduce selections from this book, write to Permissions, Walker BFYR, 175 Fifth Avenue, New York, New York 10010

Chart on page 36 courtesy of the University of Sydney

Library of Congress Cataloging-in-Publication Data
Miller, Debbie S.
Survival at 120 above / by Debbie S. Miller ; illustrations by Jon Van Zyle.
p.   cm.
Includes bibliographical references.
ISBN 978-0-8027-9813-8 (hardcover) • ISBN 978-0-8027-9814-5 (reinforced)
1. Desert animals—Australia—Simpson Desert—Juvenile literature. 2. Desert ecology—Australia—Simpson Desert—Juvenile literature. 3. Heat adaptation—Australia—Simpson Desert—Juvenile literature. I. Van Zyle, Jon, ill. II. Title. III. Title: Survival at one-twenty above. IV. Title: Survival at one hundred twenty above.
QL338.M55 2012   591.75409943'7—dc23   2011021943

Art created with acrylic on 300-lb coldpress watercolor paper
Typeset in Horley Old Style
Book design by Nicole Gastonguay

Printed in China by Hung Hing Printing (China) Co., Ltd., Shenzhen, Guangdong
(hardcover) 10 9 8 7 6 5 4 3 2 1
(reinforced) 10 9 8 7 6 5 4 3 2 1

All papers used by Bloomsbury Publishing, Inc., are natural, recyclable products made from wood grown in well-managed forests. The manufacturing processes conform to the environmental regulations of the country of origin.

ACKNOWLEDGMENTS

A very special thanks to Chris Dickman at the University of Sydney's Institute of Wildlife Research for inviting me to be a volunteer on one of their scientific research trips to the Simpson Desert. Camping in the desert allowed me to study the fascinating animals that are well adapted to this hot, dry environment. Thanks to Bush Heritage, a conservation organization that manages reserves within the Simpson Desert and supports scientific research. I'm also grateful to the Alaska State Council on the Arts for a grant that helped cover some of the travel expenses to Australia.

In the Simpson Desert there were many biologists and scientists who answered questions about desert life and who reviewed and critiqued my manuscript. Their knowledge and field experience enabled me to write this book. Many thanks to: Anke Frank, Niki Hill, Bobby Tamayo, Aaron Greenville, Tony Popic, Max Tischler, and Adam Kerezsy. Last, a heartfelt thanks to Richard Nelson, who introduced me to Australia and the wonderful group of people who study desert ecology and who also shared his great animal-sound recordings so that children can listen to the voices of the desert world.

SURVIVAL
AT
120 ABOVE

Debbie S. Miller
illustrations by **Jon Van Zyle**

Walker & Company
New York

As the night sky melts away, the Simpson Desert horizon glows like a campfire. Creaking voices of crickets grow faint. The dawn air is dry and warm when the chiming wedgebill sings its five-note song, "Time to get up now . . . time to get up now."

A brilliant sun peeks above the longest parallel sand dunes in the world. As soft as powder, the stunning sand is the color of a red brick. In early days, people called this arid land the "Great Ribbed Desert" because of the long, wind-shaped dunes that finger across Australia for hundreds of miles (hundreds of kilometers). This vast, rippled desert bakes beneath a dome of a forever-blue sky.

Reptiles stir. A sand goanna (go-AN-a) swaggers into the bright sunshine from an underground burrow. His 2-foot (61-centimeter)-long tail cuts S-turns into the velvety sand of the dune. A maze of black patterns decorates the tan skin of this large lizard. His camouflaged body blends in with the dry grasses of the spinifex. Many round humps of this needle-sharp grass cover the dunes.

The goanna's forked tongue explores the ground. Acting like a nose, the tongue discovers the scent and location of food or predators. A shiny emerald beetle scurries across the sand. Flicking his tongue, the goanna laps up a good meal of protein. Above him, a huge wedge-tailed eagle circles. The goanna detects the shadow of this predator with the tiny sensor eye on top of his head and immediately bolts into a clump of spinifex.

By noon the sand is blistering hot beneath a cloudless sky. The temperature rises to more than 120 degrees Fahrenheit (50 degrees Celsius). For seven years the desert has faced a great drought, with only an occasional sprinkling of rain. Seeds lie dormant, lacking enough moisture to sprout. During this scorching time, the goanna moves to a grove of gidgee trees. With barbed claws, he climbs a tree seeking shade and a breeze. Other reptiles tunnel beneath the sand to find cooler ground.

Near the goanna, a mob of red kangaroos rests in the shade of the trees. Some of the kangaroos lick their arms and paws to cool themselves. When a breeze drifts through the open woodland, moisture evaporates from their fur, which lowers their body temperature. The world's largest marsupial also has special hair that helps reflect sun rays. Each shiny strand acts like a tiny mirror.

In the afternoon, a blustery wind signals a change in weather. Puffy clouds run across the sky with veils of rain streaming beneath them. These misty curtains of rain, known as virga, evaporate before reaching the ground due to rising heat. The scattered clouds bring cooler temperatures and a patchwork of shade to the red sand.

At last, a few drops reach the ground, then some sprinkles. Suddenly, as though someone turned on a faucet, the light drizzle changes to pouring rain. Each drop finds a home on a grain of sand, a leathery leaf, or the fur of a kangaroo. Withered roots welcome the rain like a dry kitchen sponge. Now the desert is really wet!

Parched creek beds turn into bubbling streams, fingering across the desert. Dry claypans, wrinkled with cracks, turn into swamps. Patient fairy-shrimp eggs hatch after baking in the dry clay for seven long years. Triops erupt from this new source of life. These minnow-like crustaceans grow domed shells that look like tiny horseshoe crabs. Rainbowfish squiggle up the meandering creeks, migrating to new ponds.

Bonk . . . bonk . . . bonk. It sounds like someone is playing a distant bongo. Filling her throat pouch with air, a female emu makes a drumming sound as she strides across the open woodland. She smells water.

This huge, flightless bird looks like a grass hut walking on scaly stilts. Like an ostrich, her round body is stacked with feathers. Well adapted to the heat, her loose, open feathers allow air to pass through them. They shade and cool her body. As she moves toward the distant water, her giant three-toed feet support her in the soft sand.

While emus saunter across the dunes, herons, pelicans, and other waterbirds fly overhead. Sensing the distant rain, these birds fly hundreds of miles from the coast to feast on the explosion of life in the desert swamps. It is a mystery how these birds sense the rain, sometimes from 1,000 miles (1,610 km) away.

Wearing a spiny coat of armor, a thorny devil crawls slowly from his burrow. Only 8 inches (20 cm) long, this unique lizard looks like a miniature ankylosaurus dinosaur. The top of his body is completely covered with thorny spikes, protecting him from predators. Soon he discovers a highway of tiny black ants, his only food source. Thrusting out his sticky tongue, he devours the ants one by one. The thorny devil can eat as many as three thousand ants in one day.

Standing in a patch of wet sand, the thorny devil reveals his drinking secret. Through capillary action, this lizard can drink this water from his feet. The water moves upward along narrow grooves on the skin's surface from his toes, up his legs, to the corners of his mouth, similar to the way a plant drinks water from its roots.

A blue-tailed skink searches for a bright patch of sunshine. Darting across the sand, this striped lizard discovers a basking spot that offers a good lookout for possible predators. As the skink warms himself, a venomous western brown snake is slithering toward him.

The well-camouflaged snake draws closer, curving through the grasses. Suddenly, the skink hears a rustling sound. Immediately he begins waving his blue tail. It looks like the lizard is performing a hula dance. Attracted by the movement, the snake's head races forward. Her gaping mouth tries to bite the dancing tail. Instantly, the end of the lizard's tail breaks off, and the skink dashes away into the safety of the spinifex. The skink will grow a new tail, a special adaptation for survival. Some lizards lose and regrow their tails several times during their lives.

As the sun slips below the horizon, a peach sky deepens to the shade of strawberries. The dunes begin to cool. An Australian raven closes the day with his moaning call: *Ah . . . Ah . . . Ahhhhhhhhhh.* On cue, the voices of crickets loudly fill the air like thousands of castanets.

Nocturnal animals grow restless in their burrows. A brush-tailed mulgara (mul-GAR-uh) cautiously peeks out of an exit hole, sniffing the air. She smells the faint scent of a dingo, but no worries—the wild dog's tracks are several days old.

The mulgara has sensitive black eyes designed for night vision. In the soft moonlight this predator detects a sandy inland mouse. The quick mulgara scampers along the trail of tiny round footprints. *Pounce!* She snatches the mouse as he feeds on some dried seeds. No longer hungry, the mulgara returns to her burrow. This hamster-size marsupial plays an important role in controlling rodents and keeping the diversity of desert life in balance.

Pockets of sand begin to move. Brown heads speckled with orange spots brush through the surface of the sand. After many dormant months of rest, known as estivation, desert spadefoot frogs explode from the ground. Near midnight, hundreds of these amphibians begin cooing for their mates near the edge of a pond.

The chorus of frogs attracts other animals. White wings suddenly flash through the darkness. A spotted nightjar cuts swiftly through the air. He dives at a frog, attempting to snatch her from the ground. The warty frog quickly protects herself by secreting a milky liquid from her poison glands through the skin of her neck. When the nightjar bites the frog, this sticky white goo acts like glue. The goo cements the mouth of the nightjar so he can't eat the frog. She's a superglue frog!

The moon casts soft light on new seedlings that will turn dust bowls into lush carpets of plants.

A mouse-size dunnart (DUN-art) senses the new moisture. He scurries beyond the spinifex that shields him. Dashing quickly, he is watchful for mulgaras and other lurking predators. His ink-black, beady eyes allow him to see clearly in the darkness. This nocturnal marsupial also has a keen sense of smell. The dunnart knows the scent of rain-soaked ground means there will be more plants and many invertebrates to feed on.

Tracing the scent, the dunnart zigzags through the maze of spinifex, scurrying mile after mile to reach the swamp area. Along the way he spots the sparkling eyes of a hefty spider. He races past an emu bush and catches this midnight snack. The dunnart absorbs enough water from spiders and other prey so that he can survive without drinking water.

Through the night he journeys. His tiny feet become swollen and blistered. By the time the dunnart reaches the swamp, he will have traveled nearly 2 miles (3.2 km) during one night. Given the dunnart's short 1-inch (2.5-cm) stride, this distance would be the equivalent of a human walking 20 miles (32.2 km) in one night!

A ningaui (nin-GOW-ee) stirs. She feels the cool night air and leaves her underground home. This thumb-size creature, one of the smallest marsupials, weighs as little as six paper clips. Dashing between the spinifex, her tiny cone-shaped head and flattened ears allow her to squeeze through thick clumps of grasses. As she hunts for beetles and spiders, the sound of a running animal startles her. She spots the fleeting shadow of a doglike creature.

The panting dingo is chasing a large feral house cat. Sand flying, the sleek cat races through the obstacle course of spinifex. While the dingo is a larger animal, the wild cat is quick and nimble. He slips away, springing over bushes, escaping over the crest of the dune. The ningaui is lucky. Feral cats are fierce predators, feeding on many small marsupials and reptiles. The dingo helps control cats and other feral animals so that native species, such as ningaui and mulgara, can survive.

While the thorny devil and sand goanna rest in their burrows, a spinifex hopping-mouse scurries through a network of underground tunnels. The mouse cautiously peeks outside, then dashes toward a clump of dead grasses that camouflage him.

This nocturnal mouse hops across moon shadows, his long feathery tail arching behind him. Sniffing the cool red sand, he finds spinifex seeds. Like many other desert animals, this well-adapted mouse can take enough liquid from his food to survive without drinking water.

As night fades away, a boobook owl suddenly dives from her perch toward the mouse. The cautious mouse reacts immediately to the faint shadow of this predator. Springing off his strong hind legs, he leaps to the shelter of the spinifex.

At dawn, red kangaroos feed on fresh green shoots. They are most active during dusk and dawn when the temperatures are cooler. Creatures that like the twilight are crepuscular animals.

As one mother kangaroo grazes, her joey listens to a pair of Australian magpies singing their beautiful duet. Joining the magpies is a loud chorus of cooing frogs and creaking crickets.

Beyond the kangaroos a lone camel plods over the dune, leaving plate-size tracks in the sand. This one-humped dromedary camel can live for months without water, yet he smells the rain-fed swamp and marches toward it. Like other desert animals and plants, the camel will thrive on the gift of rain.

The desert is a sea of green and red in the early morning light. Like cresting waves, the dunes rise and fall above green swales and newly formed swamps. The endless ridges of red sand create a land similar to the wavy texture of corduroy.

The emus discover a swamp after traveling many miles. They kneel in the shallow water, splashing themselves with their stubby wings. Surrounding them are white-necked herons, avocets, and pink-eared ducks. These birds are feasting on the fairy shrimp, triops, and other aquatic invertebrates. The long seven-year drought is over. For a short time life will flourish in this vast and beautiful land of red.

AUTHOR'S NOTE

Traveling to Australia's Simpson Desert was an adventure of a lifetime. I was fortunate to camp at a research site in this remote desert with a wonderful team of scientists from the University of Sydney.

For three weeks we explored this hot, subtropical desert, which has the longest parallel sand dunes in the world. This stunning world of red sand exploded with life because of recent rains and the end of a seven-year drought. Each day we arose before dawn so we could study the animals during the cool part of the morning. Like many of the marsupials and reptiles, we rested in the shade when the scorching afternoon temperatures would climb above 100 degrees F (38 degrees C).

On my first day in the desert we saw the amazing thorny devil lizard, its scaly body covered with spikes. This fascinating creature looked like a miniature dinosaur, and I got to hold it in the palm of my hand. During our studies I helped hold, measure, and release many of the desert's well-adapted marsupials, lizards, skinks, and frogs. We watched out for dangerous snakes, scorpions, and centipedes. Each animal featured in this book I studied with my own eyes and described in my journal. I asked the scientists many questions and took photographs so that Jon Van Zyle could create the beautiful, realistic illustrations.

Life in the desert was very different from life on the arctic tundra near my home in Alaska. Yet, the desert and arctic animals have similar adaptations to survive in these two harsh environments. For example, the wood frog, described in our book *Survival at 40 Below*, freezes solid during its winter hibernation in Alaska, and Australia's desert spadefoot frog can be dormant under the sand for years during times of drought. Seeing these frogs pop out of the sand after the rains was magical!

GLOSSARY

Burrow: an underground shelter made by an animal that dug a hole or tunnel in the earth

Capillary action: the flow of liquid against gravity due to the force of molecules attracting each other

Claypan: the dry, cracked surface of a low-lying place that was once flooded with water; when these temporary ponds and lakes evaporate, a fine layer of clay sediments remain, often in the shape of a pan

Crepuscular: to be active during twilight, at dawn or dusk

Desert: a dry, arid region that typically receives less than ten inches of rain per year

Diversity: the variety of animal and plant species in an environment; the Simpson Desert has the greatest diversity of reptiles in the world

Dune: a rounded hill or ridge of sand formed by the wind

Estivation: the dormant or resting state of an animal during the hot summer or times of drought

Feral: a wild, invasive animal that can be a threat to native animals or plants of an environment

Gidgee tree: a type of acacia tree found in arid regions of Australia

Marsupial: a mammal that carries and nurses its young in a pouch; there are many different marsupials in Australia, such as kangaroos, koalas, wombats, opossums, mulgaras, and dunnarts

Nocturnal: to be active during the night

Predators: animals that capture and feed on other animals

Spinifex: a type of sharp, prickly grass that grows in round clumps in arid regions of Australia; this hardy grass provides food and shelter for many desert animals

Venomous: when an animal is able to inject a poisonous liquid venom with a bite or sting; Australia has some of the most venomous snakes in the world, including the eastern brown snake

Virga: wispy sheets of rain that evaporate before reaching the ground

⊰⇒ Record High and Low Temperatures ⇐⊱

Australia is experiencing rapid climate change related to global warming. Temperatures have risen an average of nearly 2 degrees F since the middle of the twentieth century. There are more heat waves and fewer days of frost and cold temperatures.

About 70 percent of Australia is arid, semiarid, or desert. This chart (courtesy of the University of Sydney) shows the record high and low temperatures for the Simpson Desert at Ethabuka, Queensland, near our research camp.

	Jan	Feb	Mar	Apr	May	Jun	Jul	Aug	Sep	Oct	Nov	Dec
°F	120	118	114	109	97	96	95	103	109	114	117	117
°C	49	48	46	43	36	36	35	39	43	46	47	47
°F	56	51	47	35	29	23	24	23	29	38	45	46
°C	13	11	8	2	−2	−5	−4	−5	−2	3	7	8

The highest temperature ever recorded in Australia is 123.3 degrees F, or 50.7 degrees C, at Oodnadatta, South Australia, on January 2, 1960.

Further Sources for Reading and Surfing

To learn more about Australia's deserts, visit Alice Springs Desert Park at www.alicespringsdesertpark.com.au/kids/.

To learn more about Australia's wildlife, visit the Australian Wildlife Conservancy at www.australianwildlife.org.

To compare the desert animals of the Sonoran Desert in the United States to animals of the Simpson Desert in Australia, visit www.desertmuseum.org/kids/oz.

——————————————— Read More About Deserts ———————————————

Cobb, Vicki, and Barbara Lavallee. *This Place Is Dry*. New York: Walker & Company, 1993.

Hodge, Deborah, and Pat Stephens. *Who Lives Here? Desert Animals*. Toronto: Kids Can Press, Ltd., 2008.

Wojahn, Rebecca Hogue, and Donald Wojahn. *An Australian Outback Food Chain: A Who-Eats-What Adventure*. Minneapolis: Lerner Publications Company, 2009.

To hear the voices of the Australian desert animals in *Survival at 120 Above* and to learn more about the Simpson Desert, visit the author's website at www.debbiemilleralaska.com.